MW01180743

Bed*Time*Stories

Bed*Time*Stories

By Barbara Worton

*The short, long and tall tales
of a sleepwriter*

Great Little Books, LLC
Glen Rock, New Jersey

Any dialogue or behavior ascribed to the characters in this book—those who are real people as well as characters who are imagined—is entirely fictitious.

2007 Great Little Books, LLC Hardcover Edition

Copyright © 2007 by Barbara Worton

ISBN 13: 978-0-9790661-0-8

Cover illustration by Carlos Pion
Cover and book design by Carlos Pion

Published in the United States by Great Little Books, LLC.

Publisher's Cataloging-In-Publication Data
(Prepared by The Donohue Group, Inc.)

Worton, Barbara.
  BedTimeStories : the short, long and tall tales of a sleepwriter / by Barbara Worton ; cover illustration by Carlos Pion. -- 1st ed.

  p. ; cm.

  ISBN-13: 978-0-9790661-0-8
  ISBN-10: 0-9790661-0-7

1. American literature--21st century. 2. Inspiration. 3. Authorship. 4. Creative writing. I. Pion, Carlos. II. Title. III. Title: Bedtime stories

PS3623.O78 B43 2007
818.6   2006910063

Printed in the United States of America on acid-free paper

First Edition

Amex, Armani, Baby Wipes, Bluetooth, Bloomingdale's, BMW, Bronx Zoo, Campbell's, Charmin, Chevy Suburban, Chrysler 300C, Cirque du Soleil, Clearasil, Darth Vader, Diesel, Dove, Drano, Everybody Loves Raymond, Fieldcrest, Ford Taurus, Frasier, Gucci, Hallmark, Honda Civic, Hydroflossing, Ivory, La Perla, Lestoil, Lycra, Martha Stewart, Mercs (Mercedes Benz), Meet The Press, New York Times, Post-it-Note, Prozac, Q-Tip, Ralph Lauren, Rocky, Safeguard, Stratolounger, Tour de France, Versace, Victoria's Secret, Volkswagen, Wamsutta, WeightWatchers, Will & Grace and World Wildlife Fund are all trademarks, registered or unregistered, of their respective trademark holders.

To Josephine, my mom, who read me to sleep
and introduced me to my love of books.
To Geoff, my husband, who hugs me to sleep.

Fore*word*

Sleepwriting is Barbara Worton's way of talking her-self to sleep. It's a conversation that takes place in her head. Fortunately for us, Barbara has put all that private talk down on paper. For those of us who have had the opportunity to read *Bedtime Stories*, it's actually our wake-up call. It is a call to see again, ordinary things, people and places in refreshing ways. The tales—in all kinds of forms: stories, poems, haikus—and what Barbara does, ultimately, gives us a range of emotional permission.

In "One Salty Tale" of five pickles dancing, Barbara anthropomorphosizes gherkins—of all things—and ponders the virtues and liabilities of never growing up or straying far from home. She gives us permission to be neurotic in "Broken Glass" with her overzealous focus on bacterial wipes. "Orlando" makes us wonder about changing the course of our lives and the wisdom of suddenly taking off in unimagined directions. How many times have you looked into a bowl of alphabet soup and found a message there? In "My Dinner with Barbara," she allows us to look for meaning in the bowl.

Barbara is a writer, a friend and a listener. She is every-day authentic and gives meaning to who we are. In "Enough," she gives us permission to breathe bigger than we ever thought we could, and, ultimately, when we turn the last page of her book, we are left with a smile in our minds.

—*Rochelle Udell, friend*

TABLE OF CONTENTS

EARNING *my* ZZZZZZZS

Falling asleep at just about any time—other than in the passenger seat of our car on long trips—isn't easy for me. I'm not an insomniac, just a woman with an overly developed sense of purposefulness. Every day, I need to do something other than work or take care of my house that advances my sense of self, proves that I do have a brain and is evidence that I'm a contributing member of the human race.

Should I crawl between the sheets at night without doing this, no reruns of *Everybody Loves Raymond*, *Will & Grace* and *Frasier* or a good book are going to put me to sleep. The "now I lay me down to sleep…" thing never worked for me either, too scary.

Counting sheep always leads me to counting my bills or the number of things I have to do the next day. Of course, I'm also not the type to take a pill. I have to do something to earn my rest. So, a few years ago, I started doing the thing I always say I never have enough time to do. I started writing stories just before I turned out my bedroom light, and I formally dubbed myself a sleepwriter.

My sleepwriting grew from what I learned reading *The Artist's Way: A Spiritual Path to Higher Creativity* by Julia Cameron and Mark Bryan. The book suggests three pages of non-stop writing (no going back to the beginning to edit until you reach the end) every morning.

I write my pages at night. I start each story with the first word or sentence that pops into my head and let my mind unravel and my body wind down. The daily buzz of doing things other people want me to do grows quiet. By the time I've reached my third page of writing, I put down my pen and journal, and I'm tuned down enough to fall into a deep and very restorative sleep. My dreams are vivid, and, in the morning, I wake up refreshed and my creative juices are flowing. That makes it a lot easier to sit down and write for a living—which is what I do.

The stories in this book were born from my sleepwriting. Some of the stories have been lifted directly from the pages of my notebooks, some have been edited and others expanded.

Some of these stories were written in a single night, others over the course of several days or weeks. I'd start some stories on a Monday, and on Tuesday, Wednesday, etc., my writing picked up where I'd finished the night before.

When I put *Bedtime Stories* together, I sent it around for a test-read. Friends, editors, agents, other writers and designers read it. Everyone told me my collection of stories did not put them to sleep. My sleepwriting, my mind unraveling on paper, got them thinking, going and doing. Reading what I'd sleepwritten—stories borne from deep in my subconcious—opened their minds and inspired their creative work. A lot of my readers said it helped their writing, others said it just helped them to approach their day and the things they had to do with more energy, more creativity and a sense of greater possibility. That makes me feel very good.

I hope you enjoy these stories. I recommend reading them when you need a non-toxic escape from reality, when you want to see things from a different point-of-view and if you need a little help getting yourself and your work going. My *Bedtime Stories* are very soothing and sometimes a little silly, sad, scary or sexy. And if you enjoy my stories, I recommend that you find a pen and a notebook and write your own stories. In fact, at the back of the book you'll find "How to Sleepwrite Bedtimes Stories." Give it a try. Sleepwriting feels great. It's a chance to let your mind and heart tell the stories that you need to tell, and sleepwriting is the ultimate non-toxic sleep aid. You will earn your ZZZZZZZS. ☽

Alfresco
Dining

Summer was sitting beside us in the restaurant tonight. Next table. Four kids: three girls, one boy. Family, friends, maybe brother and sister. One preteen, sweet and quiet, trying to tell the grown-ups what she thought about this and that and the other thing. One budding blonde beauty baby-sitting the other three. Lots of braces and pukka shells and tans and T-shirts and hair so shiny and clean with promise and sun and the joy of not planning for tomorrow, just laughing tonight, flirting with the future from a place of deep expectations.

Dad comes over from the grown-ups' table, strokes the youngest child's hair. A rhyming game starts, and from another table, a four-year-old chimes in, uninvited, and the summer night grows brighter. We ask for our check, pay and leave for the moon and the beach. ❯

‌A CERTAIN A‌

At a certain age, a G-string causes pain, pinches, flashes of missed opportunity, of why didn't I know this loving man when I was so perfect and free.

At a certain age, a thong bikini on a store window mannequin is a red, stinging slap, square in the soft, slackened face of mortality.

At a certain age, you can't buy what you don't know how to find, can't replace what you never had and really know insurance comes at too high a price.

At a certain age, you stop caring about who did what to whom and see all too clearly what you did to yourself. You see there's no romance in self-destruction, and you won't take *that* blame.

At a certain age, night wraps tight around your heart, stops your sleep, and you're awake, sweaty, cold and teary, just you and the terror of knowing all the roads on your map are dead ends.

At a certain age, you can't think about how great it will be when you get home, because the one thing you do know is that you don't know the way.

At a certain age, I woke up, said I'm sorry, pulled the shades tight, turned my back on my Beatles' albums and whispered, "forget peace, give me a chance."

At a certain age, I stood up, screamed and shouted, and stamped my feet at a world that says women reach a certain age. ☽

The
BES T DAY

What would I do if I woke up tomorrow and knew this will be a day unlike any other day? Perhaps this day I will put the first woman on the moon, dressed in Versace and Victoria's Secret lingerie.

After the launch, I'll fly to Brussels for brunch, bring back some beautiful baked baba-au-rhums, beer, chocolates and have a boozy tea with all my neighbors. The tea leaves will reveal great wisdom at the bottom of my cup, first a heart, then a dollar sign, then a bald eagle, and I'll know what all the symbols mean—even the eagle.

On a day unlike any other day, I would imagine everything, even the most obvious, would have new meaning. Yes would be no, and vice versa. Opposites would no longer attract. The poles would reverse, and what goes up would just keep going and going and going into the next solar system.

There would be no questions, only answers, and I would have them all. But I wouldn't be smug about it, because as wise as I am on this one day, I'd know that I was sure to forget everything tomorrow, and that wouldn't matter much anyway. I mean, what could I do with knowledge gained when birds walk and lambs fly and the cow never jumps over the moon. ☽

I have to believe I'm enough. I'm tired of waiting for it to be the right time, for the moon to be in the right house, the laundry to be in final spin, for the road to be wide open and the train on time.

I have to believe I'm enough, not two eggs short of a dozen, two bottles short of a six-pack, five pounds over-weight, two inches under height, too big, too small, too fat, too skinny, just not right.

I have to believe that I'm enough to be held, to be loved, to be cherished without condition, to be seen for who I am straight from the heart, to be heard, to be heard. Are you listening?

I have to believe that I'm enough without buying my way in, or out or up, without the sack of laundry on my back, the bags of groceries in my arms, the taxes filed and paid.

I have to believe I'm enough to be okay, to be the right choice over everything else, to be more than date night on a Wednesday, a long lunch, a few days' vacation on some dead-end trip.

I have to believe I'm enough to earn a standing ovation just because I open my eyes in the morning and get out of bed. I have to believe I'm enough. I'm so tired of waiting, and I know I'll never hear it from you. ☽

The Chrysler 300C is hot
with the hip-hop crowd and,
curiously enough, a few of the
white middle-aged guys I've
known since high school. So
hot. I see the 300C drive by,
tankish, cruising. The fat, drag-
ging-on-the-ground low-rider
bumpers. The over-sized
big-mouthed grill, like a white-
tooth diamond-studded smile.
Like a major bling-bling belt
buckle hanging low on the
belly—so low, heavy metal
perched atop a penis. Flaccid
or hard, I wonder? Is the cold,
sharp weight of that heavy
metal bling a turn-on or just
a not-so-subtle reminder that
despite the world's murderous
stares, you are a man? ☽

AUTO
EROTICA

W

L

O

B

If promises were bubbles, how high would they fly? Up to your knees? Way close to your eyes?

If promises were bubbles, would they sparkle and fly, fly and fly, soaring high?

If promises were bubbles, would they be so easily broken? Made in an instant, empty tokens?

If promises were bubbles, I'd blow quite a few and sail them across the miles between me and you.

If promises were bubbles … STOP! I can't write this story. It's too bubble-gum cute. ❯

B*i*LLBOARD

There's an enormous billboard on Broadway between 42nd & 41st Streets on a building in Times Square. Two photos of a she-hottie, dark hair, green eyes, ringed with black eyeliner, pouty red lips and rich, buttery skin that could be Italian, Puerto Rican, Jewish, Indian, Saudi.

She's wearing tight, low-cut jeans, a plunging neckline and lots of hot-off-the-boat-from-China twinkling jewelry. She's got the look that says she wants to marry a dentist who can buy her anything she wants. He'll be the son of one of her mother's friends, and they'll meet after she's dated every guy on the Upper East Side, but can't find anyone who's everything she wants him to be.

She'll marry the dentist at a huge wedding with lots of bridesmaids and let him have a free feel every now and then, and sex when she doesn't have a make-believe headache, and she'll think about his bank balance and get off.

Two photos, two poses of the she-hottie. Pose one is from the side, butt-crack, semi-visible, she's holding an ice-pick in her hand. In pose two, her breasts, lots of cleavage, are draped over an ice sculpture of the company logo, eyes fierce. And I wonder. Why? ☽

BROKEN GLASS

Men go to the dump and recycling center. That's the way it is in my town. They come in cars, trucks and SUVs, sometimes pulling trailers. They come alone and in bunches: husbands, fathers, sons, grandfathers, uncles, brothers. They haul brown paper supermarket bags stuffed to splitting with clear brown and green bottles; newspapers, milk cartons, magazines, junk mail and household rubbish that stinks from sitting in open plastic bins in overheated garages for days and days, maybe weeks.

Men in my town haul old screen windows, carpet scraps, torn curtains and tree stumps, and hoist them high over their heads and toss them into smelly dumpsters swarming with a frenzy of flies. And these men don't flinch or jump at the sound of shattering bottles, broken picture frames, mismatched glasses, chipped dishes, old pill bottles and 1970s mirrored medicine cabinets.

I quake and jump, fumble through my purse for antibacterial wipes to give my husband after he's finished dropping his load. And I observe. How many people did it take to drink all the beer that was in those bottles that guy with the backwards baseball cap and jeans which aren't hiding his butt-crack just crashed into the trash? And I see a big old car pull up and a woman who looks like she could suck snake venom right out of your leg get out. She pops the trunk and lifts out two department store shopping bags. She climbs the steps to the dumpsters, swings her bags back and forth, back and forth, and throws one then the other like a discus into the wide-open bin.

SMASH. CRASH.

The noise her rubbish makes is impressive, but lost on me. She wipes her hands on her jeans, rubs her nose and walks back to her car, I watch angry and hoping my husband didn't see this superfemale feat. I do not want "go to the dump" as the newest item on my to-do list. **〉**

D R E

A

M O N

I want to sleep a really cozy sleep. Not like a log. I don't want to wake up in the fireplace. (Big laugh and drum roll, please! It's Shecky Green!) I want to sleep as deep as a bear sleeps over the long winter months. Then I want to wake like spring—bright, colorful and full of life. I want to hear bells ring and voices carry, and I want peace on earth in my lifetime. I want to be safe and smart and fiscally responsible and sound like an angel when I sing all the songs I have been dreaming to sing. ☽

faux emily

I am delightful, delovely, deciduous. Oh, Oh. I am the falling leaves of autumn, the bursting buds of spring, the waving pampas grasses in which the birdies sing. I am a fragrant summer breeze, scents of BBQs, honey-suckle and beer, and I am going to be sick. ❯

HIGH *AnXiEty*

I worry at the stop light, when the Ford Taurus—with a mom and dad and three kids in the back seat and a "my child is an honor student" bumper sticker—that's in front of me shifts into reverse and backs up to let a Chevy Suburban pull out of a driveway and make a left turn.

I worry because the guy in the Taurus doesn't immediately shift back into drive. His white back-up lights are still on when the light turns green and the traffic starts moving, and he's talking to his kids in the back seat. I hold my breath and steering wheel tight until his back-up lights go off, and he's in drive, moving forward.

I worry when my niece sleeps over in our loft bedroom. There's a mirror hanging over the bed up there—an antique from my husband's parents, their wedding gift. Will the chain give out? Will it fall? I don't know, so I take it down and sleep all night with the bedroom door open and the light on. ❯

I wish I could forget the flute player. He had skinny lips, chapped and flat, from pursing to blow clear, round, fairy-light tones. One day, we were on the roof, tanning. He was so white and kind of doughy, and his hair wasn't blonde or brown, just greasy and hard to look at. So I stared straight ahead, over my bikini and down my tan legs stretched out on my Peter Max towel to my feet.

Shock! Horror! Embarrassment!

My pedicure was chipped, both big toes. Quick, I sat up and tucked my feet under my butt, like one of those Asian women so often photographed in rice paddies, and placed my hands over my feet. I realized, too late, that the flute player thought I'd changed position to pay more attention to him, to get flirty. I knew this because he tilted his head so his greasy hair fell over his steel frame glasses, and he lunged at me. I rolled left, fast enough to slide into the open roof hatch and bump down the ladder, butt hitting each rung. I hit the ground running, and by the time he caught up with me, I was in the kitchen in a kaftan, drinking a diet soda, my feet in slippers. ❩

feet first

23

f oo d

fetish

Now I lay me down to sleep. I pray the Lord my soul keep. If I die…

No way.

No way.

Now I lay me down to sleep. I pray the Lord to stop my stomach from aching, to stop this craving and to stop my mouth from eating cookies, big fat chocolate chip cookies.

I look like a whale. I lie here, and I can feel this big stomach of mine, and I am disgusted. Really disgusted.

Pig. Pig. Pig. I couldn't pass on the chips, stop at one cookie?

Tomorrow. Tomorrow. Tomorrow.

Creeps on in its petty pace (Oh my God, this is another Shakespearean tragedy) to the last 2,000-calorie meal. Why do I keep eating when I feel bloated, fat, disgusting?

Who is the patron saint of Weight Watchers, and why isn't she answering my prayers? Okay, tomorrow. I'm seriously back on my diet.

No bread. No carbs at all. None!

But...

I don't want to freak, so maybe I should cut back slowly.

Only one cookie. No wine. Well, maybe wine and no cookie or bread. Or maybe...

I'll just wire my jaw. ☽

HE HAS RISEN

I don't get it. There you were. Stuck in your Stratolounger, remote in one hand, soda in the other. You sat and watched TV, volume turned jackhammer high. So loud you couldn't hear me and didn't have to talk to me, and when you tried, I just wanted to scream. Then the earth shook and steamed and parted, birthing a huge oozing hole, and finally you rose. ❯

if Only

I was on the 6th Avenue bus a few weeks ago. I was sitting in the "please give this seat to the elderly or disabled" seat. I'd earned it.

My left foot was in a cast, fractured by a pound of chopped meat that had fallen out of my freezer. My right hand was in a brace, repetitive stress disorder from too much keyboarding. I reeked of arnica, and I was carrying a briefcase, laptop, handbag and umbrella.

I was just looking out the front window of the bus, while people looked down at me with disgust—until they saw my foot. All of a sudden, this bicycle messenger in front of the bus hit a moon-crater pothole. The front wheel of his bike crumbled, he let go of the handlebars and sailed over the collapsing bicycle, tucked, flipped in mid-air, and landed on his feet with his arms raised like Rocky. And I screamed, "Wow, if only I could do that."

If only soft, white, embarrassed to be middle-aged me could go out and even buy the courage to ride a bike in the city, never mind sail over potholes.

If only I could pick up the shattered pieces of my bicycle while horns blared and feel no need to hurry so a million drivers could get home in time to eat TV dinners.

Our Father, who art in heaven, if only hallowed could be my name.

If only I could understand why I do so many of the things I do before I do them, and then not be afraid afterwards that I didn't do the right thing and did it the wrong way.

If only I could finish the personal renovation work I started about 20 years ago. People are sick of listening to me talk about how hard it is to change.

If only I could forget the day my left breast got itchy in 9th grade art class, and in front of Drew and Pete and Joey, I was dumb enough to scratch it.

If only I could squelch the urge to tell the truth when anybody asks me, how are you?

Twinkle, twinkle little star, if only I knew where the hell you are.

If only I could care less whether you like me, think I look good, would like to get to know me and were honestly interested in hearing what I had to say.

If only the hills really were alive with the sound of music.

If only I could wear sequins and wave a skinny gold statue on national TV and say, "I'd like to thank my mother, father, sister, brother, sister-in-law, brother-in-law, all my friends, most of all my husband, without them none of this would have been possible—and skip right over the Jesus reference—and not run out of time before I forgive, notice and thank me.

If only I could skid over that moment when I fell asleep behind the wheel of my Honda Civic, when I can't deny what might have been, when I should have backed up, slowed down, stopped and said, I love you.

Bless me Father, for I have sinned, and if only I believed it was time for me to stop confessing. ❯

*infra*STRUCTURE

I'm not sure about the Lincoln Tunnel, a tile here, a tile there picked clean off the wall.

I'm not sure about the first glass of water you get in that too busy coffee shop on the corner of Fifth and Second. It comes straight to the table from that cloudy water glass and lunch tray tower that's been standing behind the counter all day.

I'm not sure about wearing shorts on the subway and taking a seat.

I'm not sure about taking the *New York Times* off the top of the stack outside the newsstand.

I'm not sure just how clean the toilet is in a house where everybody is so organic they don't use Lestoil to wash the floor.

But I'm really not sure that when I step down, the sidewalk will meet my feet. I'm not sure. I've got a history in this city. ❯

THE LITTLE COUNTRY

Once upon a time, there was a tiny country small enough to fit in a teacup. It was kind of a country inside a country with hills and roads and beaches and about 100,000 people so tiny I had to wonder... Do they have cars? And who makes their clothes and shoes? ❯

MAYBE

Maybe I could look a little uglier today. Maybe this zit that's growing on the side of my nose, growing faster than the national debt, will get even redder and bigger than the state of Georgia. Maybe I'll blow my nose, and in the process, this zit the size of a satellite dish will burst.

And maybe I'll be sitting in a meeting with some CEO in a $3,000 Armani suit, and all he'll be looking at is this zit exploded on my face and then down at my hands—and not at my boobs—and then anywhere else but my face.

But maybe, just maybe, I'll clean up real fast, without him noticing, and leave the meeting with my gooey tissue, shaking hands, bagging the deal, a spring in my step, glint in my eye.

Maybe I'll forget how cute I was before my childless belly took on a hormone-crazed, zit-growing life of its own. Maybe I'll forget all the chores and take off for the beach, check in my pocket, work on someone else's mind, estrogen and Clearasil in my suitcase. Maybe, just maybe. ❯

LUGGAGE

It took me years to get out of the house. I packed my bags and repacked just because I realized I'd forgotten a few this and thats, and I wasn't sure what I would really need. I never had hit the open road on my own before, so didn't know if it was best to pack everything I had or leave behind some clothes, shoes, coats, boots, hats, scarves, makeup, medicine and toys that didn't fit anymore.

So I stuffed too much raggedy stuff in too-big sizes and stuff so long out of style it was back in fashion again into a bag that was too small. Sleeves and cuffs, legs and buttons, collars and belt hoops popped out the top and sides, and I couldn't get this too-full, too-heavy bag off the floor and out the door.

So I went back and unpacked and packed again, and changed my clothes and my hair and my name. And checked for my passport, wallet, tickets and keys. Then I was ready, really ready, until you told me there are entrances and exits through which I will never go. ❯

Merc^i

I bought four cards for Mother's Day: two for friends, one for my sister and one for my sister-in-law. I thought about buying cards for my three aunts, but I couldn't, and I didn't buy one for you.

Nowhere to send it.

No known address.

This coming Sunday, I'll just have to sit here and think real hard. You know, send out vibes, and maybe you'll hear me. I'll dial into the cosmic consciousness and please, please, please, you'll answer my call. Maybe you'll hear me say I love you, but I don't know.

You're really gone. You were ready to go, had fought so hard to stay for me, had even warned me that you were getting ready to call it quits.

But it has been quite a while now since you left. I didn't know how much I'd miss you when you were gone, how much I'd wish I could hear you asking me if I'm okay, telling me again and again to be careful, calm down, don't worry.

You've made your point.

Are you ready now to come to me in my dreams? When I least expect it, to tap me on the shoulder? To stop a bus speeding my way? I need to know you're up there, watching over me, hearing me tell the world that I know I am the best of you and some of the worst of you. I need to know you've heard me say thank you. ❥

NO
ANSWER

Where the hell are you? I've been calling you morning, noon and night. No answer at the Long Island number.

You're not at your mother's in Brooklyn.

The phone just rings and rings when I call the record store.

The receptionist at your office at the insurance company, it's her first day on the job and she hasn't a clue where I might find you.

I called the old house and the new house in Florida. I even called your neighbors, your best friend and that tourist place where you used to volunteer.

No answer.

I don't even get your answering machine. And when someone does answer my call, and I ask for you, they slam down the phone.

Where are you? What did you do? Are you in some kind of trouble?

I woke up last night and thought maybe I'd scrambled your phone numbers. Then I remembered I hadn't tried your cell phone. I called.

No joy.

I swapped your numbers around, switched area codes, seven-digit numbers, dialed backwards, inside out.

But nothing.

Where are you? Come on. I need to talk to you. ☽

Our Bed

This bed is too big. Even at my chubbiest, this bed doesn't wrap around me, comfort me, hold me tight when you're not here, not snoring, not generating heat that warms me to my soul.

This bed is a little rumpled. The sheets on your side don't stay put. You toss and turn and wrinkle. I sleep neat and cool, not sweaty and fussy. My side of the sheets stay put and smell of lavender laundry detergent—only the organic brand—and fresh.

Sorry Martha, Ralph, Fieldcrest and Wamsutta.

Let these week-old sheets wrinkle, rumple and smell just-like-you sweet. I won't change the sheets until you come home and this bed fits just right for you and me. ❥

meanies

Blue meanies, green, pink, purple and puce.

Plaid meanies of every tartan and of every stripe. They're everywhere, except where I want them to be when I want them to be there.

Meanies in the morning, at lunch and in the evening too.

Rude little fat and skinny meanies too. Rushing here, rushing there, getting absolutely nowhere, lost in a big, ugly puddle of yuck.

Meanies, meanies, sucking air out of the room and wind out of my sails.

Meanies, meanies, cruising down the beach on the towline of a powerboat, a pyramid of meanies, very Esther Williams.

Fat-bottomed, pointy-headed meanies, grimacing with two rows of perfectly white blood-stained teeth.

Flesh-eating meanies in hula skirts, cannibal meanies on surfboards, barreling into shore, like so much pollution, washing up like oil spills.

Spoiler meanies, eat my dust meanies, meanies, meanies, meanies, everywhere, and not one of them will stop and say hi to me. ☽

Oceans[1]

If I had a boat carved from a bar of soap, with a toothpick mast and boasting a Post-it-Note sail, how far could I float before my boat bubbled up and dropped me into hot water?

I guess it depends on the brand of soap and the size of the bar. A family-sized 99 $^{94}/_{100}$% pure Ivory would certainly take me farther than a sensitive skin Dove, but I bet not as far as a supersize, family Safeguard or one of those grande French- or Italian-milled bars with extra virgin olive oil, almonds, lavender or cocoa. ❯

What do the Seven Dwarfs know that I don't? How is it that those seven really short guys, whose names I can never remember, can grab their picks, axes and shovels, and head down into a deep hole and whistle while they work?

I don't understand it. Perhaps it's just the satisfaction of backbreaking labor. Do they feel good when they're aching and in agony at the end of the day, knowing that they have chipped one more millimeter closer to the earth's cortex?

I wonder, even if they picked and axed and carted their coal out of the earth in deep, deep buckets, will they ever get to the center of things? ☽

MINIMUM
wage

Not Likely

In the dream, I'm on a train platform, with a new haircut all big, shaggy and very Brooklyn, and I'm kissing John Denver, or at least someone who looks and talks and walks like John Denver and claims he comes from somewhere corny, wheaty and flat: somewhere in the middle of the country where people have God-Fearing values and not much "I need those Gucci's" credit card debt.

I'm on the way home to my parents, and I'm telling this guy with straight, floppy, not quite blonde hair that kind of blends into his inside of a potato colored skin, sucking-on-lemon lips and aluminum aviator glasses, that he should come home with me because my parents are cool, and they'd let him sleep over in the same bed with me.

And even in my sleep, for the first time in my life, I really think I'm crazy. ☽

one salty tale

Five baby pickles all in a row. Dill mini gherkins dancing heel to toe. One step forward. Two steps back. All of these gherkins dancing tap, tap, tap.

Kick to the left. Kick to the right. Five baby gherkins fight, fight, fight.

Shake a little tail feather, wiggle and bounce. Five baby gherkins ten cents an ounce.

Five baby gherkins in a pickle parade. Five baby gherkins sweet as lemonade.

Five baby gherkins working on a tan. Five baby gherkins and none of them a man.

Buy them from the barrel ... buy them in a jar, wrap them up in plastic bags and take them in the car.

When it's time for lunch, serve them on a plate, but it's probably not smart to eat them on a date.

Five baby gherkins garlicky to the max might get a would-be Romeo the axe.

Tasty when you eat them, that gherkin taste does linger. Eat them with your breakfast and you'll be tasting them for dinner.

Five baby gherkins with the life span of a gnat went in the jar straight from the vat. Haven't been anywhere-but soaking in brine. Doesn't sound to me like a very fun time.

Five baby pickles all in a row. Dill mini gherkins dancing heel to toe. One step forward. Two steps back. All of these gherkins dancing tap, tap, tap. ♪

Orland$O$

Five cows rang my doorbell last night, about 9:00 p.m. I know it was cows, five of them, because when the bell rang, I looked in the peephole before opening the door, and there they were, all big and bovine.

One had a bell around her neck. The other had a flower tucked behind her ear, two were for all intents and purposes cow-naked, and one was wearing a hula skirt.

I opened the door and asked, "What can I moo for you?" I thought that was pretty funny. The cows didn't hoot and laugh. The one in the hula skirt yawned, and the other four just gave me these really tired grins.

"We're here collecting for the Friends of Cows Retirement Farm."

I looked at them at a 45-degree angle. "Excuse me, but don't cows live on farms all their lives? Why do you need to raise money for a retirement farm?"

The cows snorted, and it was an ugly sound. "Yeah, you think it's easy being put out to pasture?"

Honestly, I did, but I didn't want a lactose-crazed mob of two tons of beefcake breaking down my door. "Can't honestly say," I answered. "But don't you have a 401(k)? All those years of producing milk, butter, cheese and ice cream, and you don't get profit-sharing? Sounds pretty chintzy to me."

The cows said nothing, just batted their big wet, rubbery eyes and shuffled, and I knew I had to do something before there were cow pats in my hallway. "Do you have a tax exempt card?" I asked. "I need to know if you're an accredited charity. It makes a difference at the end of the year. The IRS is a stickler for receipts."

The one with the hula skirt picked up her skirt. There was a bag underneath. I reached inside and thankfully only pulled out the Tax ID. Then I asked, "So, what are you looking for? An acre of good grass? A heated spot in the barn?"

"One-way transportation to the Greater Orlando area," said the one in the hula skirt—clearly the front cow—and the naked and the bell cows agreed. "We have a friend down there, and he says the life is easy, and the weather gives you another ten years."

I started doing the math. Pound for pound this trip wasn't going to be cheap, unless of course they went as beefpatties, but that would have been defeating their purpose. "What do you need?" I asked.

"Another $1,500," the hula cow said.

It seemed like a suspiciously round number, but I went for my checkbook. "The Cow Retirement Farm" I wrote in the pay-to line. $1,500 in the amount line—words and numbers—and proudly signed on the signature line.

I grinned and handed my hard-earned check with a really nice sunset pattern and two kittens over to the hula cow. Pound for pound, $1,500 was a small price to pay.

"Thank MOO," said the hula cow with this look that said, see, we're buds.

"No thank you," I said, enunciating clearly so that there was no question who was standing on his own two feet.

Hula cow looked at the check, held it up to the light, turned it over, gave it a snappy little pull and handed it to the naked cow. She took a close look at the check, reached into some hidden pocket—don't know where, like I said, she was naked, and I don't know any naked thing, except a kangaroo, with a pocket—and she pulled out a cell phone and scanner. This cow had Bluetooth technology. She ran the scanner across the numbers and barcode on the bottom of my check.

"Do you have two forms of ID?" Hula cow asked. "One with a photo, please. A driver's license or passport will do."

"Now…"

"We can't be too careful these days. Terrorists are everywhere," Hula cow said, before I got to "wait a minute."

I took a real long time pulling out my wallet and searching through all the pockets for my license and health insurance card. Hula cow looked at the photo, looked at me, checked out the address on my house and the street sign on the corner, then handed the check to one of the naked cows and the ID back to me.

Then we all stood there. There were a lot of eyes looking this way and that way, but never making contact. Bell cow cleared her throat. It had been a long time since she'd said anything.

"Ever been to Orlando with a cow, boy?" she asked, and the naked cows started jumping up and down, and the hula cow ran off, and the bell cow started mooing at the moon, and out of nowhere pulled out a cowboy hat, string tie and a pair of six shooters.

"We're heading down for rodeo season. Big show in Kissimmee," Hula cow said. "Yeah, and even five smart cows like us will need a front man. Want to hit the road?"

We talked dollars and days off and came to terms. I went inside and packed every plaid shirt and pair of jeans I had, turned off the lights and water, and locked the doors, hitched my 2005 BMW to the back of the cow's RV, and we were off, driving south to Orlando. Yes, sir, I was on the road, me and five old cows all looking for a new beginning. ☽

My Dinner with Barbara

I had dinner with myself. Last night. In the dream. I sat down at a table in the Tate Modern in London, not the old museum but the new one on the South Bank, the converted power station, the building that's better than the art.

I sat down at a table with two other women, both about my age, both kind of blonde and tall and cute and thin-ish, but getting on in years. In England, strangers share. Even table space is limited.

The two women at my table are friends, writers. One writes mysteries, the other literature—the heavy stuff—two of my favorite genres. I eavesdropped, listened, wondering who they were, what they were working on, trying really hard not to be the nosey American outsider. I stared at my soup, like it would reveal some kind of message, but it wasn't Campbell's Alphabet.

I looked up and smiled, one of those tight-lipped, broad smiles that says, please, please, please, I have something to say, but I'm sure you're too busy to want to hear it.

Literature looked straight through me. Mystery smiled. I said, "I couldn't help but overhear what you were talking about." They smiled back, accepting the interruption and the inevitable—the outsider is coming in.

"I'm a writer too," I said, then boasted about my children's book currently under consideration and my story just published. "What do you write?" I asked, and they rattled off some titles, and I didn't know them, so I asked another question. "What are your names? I'd like to pick up some of your work."

"Barbara Worton," they both answered, and I gasped.

"Oh yes, I've heard of you."

Last night, I slipped into the sheets and closed my eyes and let go of my grip on the 9–5, the food shopping and the piles of laundry stacked up in the corner. I tossed and turned and dreamed and dreamed. I woke up confused and didn't understand, until I got on the subway in the morning, that last night I dreamed I sat down to dinner with my dream. ☽

THE PRICE *of* OKAY

Jack's dead. You called and told me. "Did you read it in the *New York Times*?" you asked.

"No. I steer clear of the obits," I answered. Who's gone and who's left behind is news I don't read.

"It was kidney disease," you told me. You've heard from the family. "Are you driving up to the memorial service?"

"No," I answered, surprised you would even ask. "Wasn't invited, or to his retirement party. You?"

"Yeah, he was a friend."

"He was my boss," I said, setting boundaries. "My uncle died of kidney failure. How are Jack's wife and kids?"

"Not good. But not surprised. He was sick for a long time." You sound tired. "Not much of a retirement, hey? If you're interested, the family is soliciting donations for the Kidney Foundation."

"Sure." I expected this. "What's the info?"

You read off the URL. I write it down.

"Do you think Beth knows?"

"Not sure," I answered. "I'll call her. Listen, at the service, say hi to everyone for me."

"Everyone, or just our friends?"

"Oh, everyone," I laughed. "It will worry them."

I call Beth and get, "Oh, too bad. Jack, my Jack. I was his pet."

It's true, so I mention the fund, and she stops me at "I have the Kidney Foundation's address."

"Can't do it," she snapped. "I have no dough."

After work, alone in my little writer's office, I keyboard in a note to Jack's family. Funny, Jack never even used an electric typewriter, I think, while my ink jet printer spits out my professional condolences. Then I write an overly generous check.

A kidney doesn't come cheap. But I suspect a generous

donation is the least I can do. Jack's dead, after all. An old boss, openhanded with perqs for junior writers—a client trip here, a Broadway show there. Research, honestly. You can, after all, only write about what you know. Jack's dead, only five years after retirement to one of those towns where all the pension plan and profit-sharing and the other 401(k) multimillionaires go.

It's a good cause, I tell myself. Lives will be saved, and for ten seconds, his family will scratch their heads and ask, "Who's this letter from? Do you remember her? I'm not sure Jack ever mentioned her."

Then they'll ask other friends from the office, and one or two will remember, and, for another ten seconds, they'll share, "Yeah, she was a junior writer, sat across the hall, a nervous girl, pretty hair. This check is a nice gesture. I guess she's doing okay." ☽

The
Rest *of*
MyLife

I woke up alive, surviving a cancer I didn't know had been growing slowly just southeast of my navel for all of my years. Now, at night, I poke my belly, just to be sure there's nothing growing, nothing out of place. I know the landscape of my tummy well. And I wonder, since I survived, what am I supposed to do with the rest of my life?

Best to go shopping, purchase some much-needed nothing, then work like an indentured slave to earn the money to pay the Amex bill. But it's not really Bloomingdale's I need, it's the Hallmark store, the big one. They seem to have a card for almost everything. I wonder, is there a you lucky sucker card?

One thing for sure: I had better start Hydroflossing my teeth twice a day. If I've got another fifty years ahead of me, I'd better do what it takes to hold on to my teeth. ⟩

The Rules

I am setting down guidelines, rules, the law. No bull. I mean it. I've had it. There are no more excuses, reasons why, and I'm not taking the hit on this one, the blame for leaving up the toilet seat, for looking at you cross-eyed, for having to keep my mouth shut to keep the peace.

Spin the bottle. Where will it land? Or will it spin out of control?

I have been carrying the world on my back, and if you don't like the way I've been shifting the load, you'd better start carrying your weight. My arms are too tired. It's all too much, but it never seems to be enough to really matter. ❯

ǝpᴉsdՈ Down

If I wake up tomorrow and up is down, black is white, yes is no, stop is go and round is square, just what will I do? Will I know when and where to cross the street, when to sit and when to stand? Would I really be able to walk on my own two feet or would I have to stand on my hands? And could I honestly hold my legs straight up over my head?

My abs aren't that great, and my feet are heavy when they're in shoes, and in the winter, I can't go without shoes. Which leads me to wonder, what would I wear on my hands while they're down in the dirt, on the side-walk or tiptoeing through the tulips. And would I have to petition Nancy Sinatra to go back into the studio to rerecord "These Extra Strong Yet Flexible Gloves Are Made for Walking?"

Imagine what all this handwalking is going to do with my miserable case of carpal tunnel syndrome. All that weight on my wrists cannot be good.

Heels over head walking is certainly going to require a different sort of bra. Right? My breasts would fall out of the beautiful, but not sensible or heavily constructed La Perla I have now.

And what about a coat? This new way of walking is going to turn fashion on its ear. Stand on my hands, and my coat will flop over my eyes, so would a lot of my clothes—dresses, blouses. Designers would have to get very creative with snaps, drawstrings and reverse suspenders. Of course, none of this would be an issue if the world dressed in lycra workout wear. But then, what about that extra weight. If I stand on my head, will my spare tire or love handles fall down around my ears and shoulders?

My hair! I'd have to cut it very short, otherwise it would drag along the street and the floor, and every day would be a bad hair day. Which leads to another worrisome business, how would I wash, bathe or go to the toilet? In the shower, I could drown, unless, of course, I take matters in hand and learn all over again how to straighten up, show some spine, flex my muscles and stand on my own two feet. ☽

rub-a-dub-dub

Rub-a-dub-dub, one girl in the tub, Me. And it's one of those big, deep, claw-footed tubs used by princesses and cowboys in Hollywood movies, filled with steaming hot water—hot enough to turn me into an undercooked chicken, inside of a bunny's ear, delicate new rose.

Rub-a-dub-dub, pink bubbles—lightly scented by some essence that won't give me hives—float up to my chin and make it safe for me to look down and see the parts of my body I want to see—toes and knees and breasts clear peaks of suds—and I survey my landscape and dream.

Rub-a-dub-dub, everything's good in the tub—not too fat not too skinny round and floaty and slide out of your hands slippery and slinky.

Rub-a-dub-dub, waiting for you to step into the tub that's so big we sit side by side, just touching where we want to touch, unconcerned about scratching this or that on the faucet or that little lever that we pull up to lock water in the tub, floating around this body part or that, not too hot or too cold for any body part to be up to the job, unworried that the porcelain will be hard on my knees and your back.

Rub-a-dub-dub, we float in the tub that's as wide and deep as the pool in our basement, but without the security cameras. I swim to you and you swim away, to the shallow end away from the water jets, and stand with your back against the tiles and your arms out wide, side-to-side, and I catch you every way I can. ❯

S U P E R

man

You slumber, close to the edge of the bed, strong, round, warm, sweet as Easter Bunny chocolate. I scribble with fine tipped pencil in the 99th notebook to live beside my side of our bed. Three pages. The very least I can do if I'm going to call myself a writer.

From some place between here and nod, you plead, "Please turn off the overhead light."

My hand is not ready to stop moving. You wait. I finish. Get up, walk past the bureaus, the laundry basket, enter the alarm code, switch off the light. Shuffle back to bed, snatching the remote control.

Click on, channel-up to reruns of old sitcoms, never the 11 p.m. news. Terrorists, murderers, politicians—any party, any country—and celebrities are banned from my bedroom. I'll only watch for a few minutes, I swear to myself, until I start to drop off to sleep.

You flip to the other side, a large, disgruntled pancake flop. You say, "I think I'm going to get you infrared headphones."

I lower the television volume to barely audible. It hardly matters, I know this show by heart. Before it's over, I sign off, pound my pillows into a shape that will support my neck, nestle my head and let me spoon close to you.

You lift your arm, and I hug you from behind, conforming to your curves. You pull me closer, and I hang on tight, clutching on to your willingness to give into sleep, and you mumble, "Yes, everything's going to be okay."

Safe, I drift off and wake only when I'm too warm and my hand is numb from the weight of your arm. I pull my tingling arm free, stretch onto my back, one hand and leg always touching you, and I smile. This is good. This is love. ☽

Rubber

Duckies

Eight rubber duckies sit at the foot of my bathtub—four girls and four boys; two devils, two Indians, two bikers, one bride and one groom. They're my tubtoys, waiting for the son and daughter I never had, waiting for my inner brat to come out to play.

My ducks, I have decided, are in committed relationships. I never match an Indian with a devil or a bride with a biker. The lady who cleans for me, however, she doesn't care about how I organize my ducks on the marble seat. She picks them up, washes them off—I never let them in the water—and puts them back in two not-very-neat rows and never matches them with the right partners. She is a single mother, angry at men, gone off relationships.

After a casual flirtation between the time the cleaning lady leaves and I get home from work, however, my ducks are kind of jumpy, eyes looking left and right and down, but not at me. So I move them back to their usual places and smile uncertainly.

Could my ducks be swingers? Maybe their devotion

is all a front? How do I know they're not carrying on with the two glow-in-the-dark ducks that sit under my bedside lamp? How do I know my bathroom isn't the scene of regular duck-swapping?

Have I the right to judge? Have I imposed my values on these poor ducks? What am I to do if my rubber ducks aren't the ducks I always believed them to be? Are they ducks of a different color, a different stripe, X-rated ducks? Does the cleaning lady know? Does she have a camcorder in her mop handle? Is she selling the tapes of the seedy goings-on in my bathroom? Is she making pots of money off these petro-chemical derived rubber duckies with cute faces and blank stares that mean whatever I want them to mean? ☽

What's this?

I'm packing.

For what?

I'm going. Don't ask me where.

What did you take?

Nothing.

Wait. Those are my shoes.

Where?

Here, underneath my coat.

No.

Yes, I can see them.

No matter.

What?

No matter. You're not going anywhere.

Oh, you know that?

Yes, I do.

How can you be so sure?

I have your keys. ♪

Packing

13

Days of Rain

One morning, very early, dawn broke and the sky grew brighter. The alarm clock chimed—no buzz, no screaming rock 'n' roll DJ—just three melodious chimes, like God was ringing the doorbell.

Joanie opened her eyes and stretched and thought about the work that would fill her day and stretched again and wished she was the type of person who could roll over and fall back to sleep and forget that responsibilities were calling—loud and clear.

But Joanie had calls to make and money to earn, and there were always so many bills to pay. So she got up. Slowly. Walked down the hall to the bathroom. Her house looked supernaturally sunny—almost like the inside of some lemon-orange hybrid, a color that she'd never seen before, a color that doesn't exist in nature.

Joanie walked into the kitchen and peeked out the window, and instead of the sun, there was this big lemon-orange yellow smile in the sky, and it started to talk. Very unnatural.

"Today," the giant lips mouthed, parted and revealed two rows of perfect white-hot teeth, "is your day. No work. All play. No worries. You won't lose your job, and you won't run out of things to do.

"Today you're safe from all the fears that keep you from doing all the things you want to do. Surf," the sunny mouth said. "Play the piano. Ice skate. Ski. Sing at the Met. Dance at Lincoln Center. Bike the Tour de France. Tumble with Cirque du Soleil. For the next twenty-four hours, you can do it all. Tonight, when you come to bed, you'll sleep a deep and very satisfied sleep."

Well, Joanie thought, I'd better take a shower. I want to start this day ready for anything. So she scrubbed and scrubbed, pouffed her hair, and moisturized head-to-toe, and did her makeup just right, and stepped into fashion-able but comfortable clothing that would get her through any velvet rope and headed for the front door.

Woo. The wind was hungry the day the sun came out as a big smile. Not a just give me a little snack, I feel like a nosh hungry, but blow your way right through the refrigerator and eat everything that hasn't molded into some past-the-purchase date, green-grey hungry.

The wind blew so hard that trees bent almost in half and telephones rang, even when there was no call coming in, and laundry whipped around clotheslines so tight that there was no telling a T-shirt from a bedsheet. All the laundry hugged the line like moths in giant cocoons.

The wind blew and blew then blew some more until the smiling sun mouth was a tight, tight, pissed-off frown. Then it opened, stretched and opened wider and wider and wider until in one giant gulp, it swallowed the wind. The air calmed down, and the clouds stood still, and the earth gave a little stress-releasing shudder and seemed to spin a little easier.

Everything was still and seemed so safe, so safe that Joanie opened the windows and the doors and stepped outside to see if the picnic table was still standing or if the dog house had blown up to the roof. And she looked up to the sky.

The sunny mouth in a color Joanie had never seen before was a mess, twisting, smirking, quivering, puckering, grimacing, stretching this way and that. The top lip popped out, was sucked in. A little blast of wind escaped, and the mouth slammed shut tight, clamped down, struggling against the wind punching around inside.

The mouth held and held and held its breath, but in one fierce eruption, it burst open, and the wind heated by those white hot lips and teeth blew out wild and steamy, and it started to pour and pour. And the sunny mouth, drop-dead exhausted, disappeared, and the sky turned grey.

Joanie slammed closed windows and doors and hunted down an umbrella and changed her shoes and pulled on a slicker, and slowly, looking left and right and up and down tiptoed out the door.

And it poured and it poured, and then it poured some more. It poured for 13 days. And it was a good thing, because the world needed a bath. The whole damn planet needed one giant scrubdown—if possible with a loofah, a scrub brush, one of those skin buffers. And a scraper, the kind pedicurists use on heels, wouldn't have hurt at all.

This planet was filthy. If there was a Q-Tip big enough, this planet needed its ears cleaned and bellybutton delinted. A good floss wouldn't have hurt either nor a flush of the eyeballs. And it would be really good if there were a giant box of Baby Wipes or millions of rolls of Charmin handy. Oh, and a spritz of organic air-freshener, maybe something in a fresh parsley or key lime.

A good soaking rain would help, but 13 straight days?

After 13 straight days of wet, Prozac sales were through the roof. People felt put-upon, damp, down-trodden, dreary, tired and fed up with wearing sensible, waterproof shoes. Would they ever wear their flip-flops or show off their pedicures again?

It was time to let the sun shine in and to come out of the shade. But there were issues and considerations. The umbrella market was up, way up. Factories in three third-world countries were running 24/7 and their economies were back on the map. Thanks to the downpour, they'd repaid their share of the third-world debt. Populations were smiling.

The IMF was flush. People were eating. Dentists were flying to remote outposts to extract molars and bond bad bicuspids and set diamonds in incisors because money was flowing like water because water was flowing like nothing that had ever been seen before.

It was funny because it was the best of times during the worst of times, and there was absolutely nothing anyone could do about the weather. Water was backing up the drains and filling the trash cans, and Joanie wasn't sure that the flowers would ever be the same again.

Where was the sun? The big, round, yellow sun.

Joanie was one pissed-off chick. Her magical twenty-four hours had come and gone 13 times, and in all the rain clouds, there was no silver lining, just lots of water and questions still unanswered. Do tornadoes really pick people up off their feet and spin them around and land them in another place? If they did, would Joanie be moved? Would she find her Garden of Eden? After the storm, would she miss the things she lost or those she never had?

And if the sun came out again, a big grinning smile, spread from one end of the sky to another, and if she was sunbathing in the nude, Joanie wondered, lying on her stomach, would the sun reach down from the sky and kiss her fifty-plus-year-old butt? Would those white-hot teeth bite her? Hmmm. Tough question, Joanie thought, then shrugged. It all depends, she decided, on whether the sun values experience. ❭

WATER WORKS

Jeans shrink in hot water. Why can't I? Imagine. One long shower in the morning, instead of a sensible breakfast and exercise. A shower after each of my three square meals and dessert—just a short shower to conserve water—and I could shrink from fat to curvy/skinny and stay that way for the rest of my life. Thin legs, nipped waist, flat abs, stick arms and two perky C-cups. Drip, drip, drip, the fat goes down the drain. I won't worry about clogging the pipes—better the fat is in those arteries than mine. Anyway, there's Drano and plumbers, and that's easier and cheaper and a lot more satisfying than dieting.↲

rOadside Attraction

I saw three bears in the woods. No kidding. I saw a momma bear, a poppa bear and a baby bear in the woods that runs beside the back road on the trip south to Cape May. It was somewhere around Freehold, New Jersey. No kidding.

The three bears didn't move and didn't growl, but I knew they were fierce. Just sitting there, they were so big and furry that I could hear their honey-poaching, berry-pinching roar.

I can't believe I'm the only one who saw those bears. The traffic was pretty heavy with cars packed with Moms and Dads and 2.2 kids and the occasional dog. Chevys, Fords, BMWs and Mercs, and more than a few Volkswagens.

It was Dad's job to drive, and the kids' job to fight, and Mom's job to look left and right and front and center for cars cutting in and out from the other lane or wild animals that just might stand up on their hind legs and bolt straight for the car with can-opener claws ready to slice open the roof and eat the whole family for lunch. Three furry bears by the side of the road, kind of cute, not moving, but from what I heard on the news, fierce and fast enough to chew up carloads of people and lick their bones clean before the New Jersey State Police even got, never mind responded to, the 911 call. ☽

TRANSFOR*me*R

I am not Andrew Lloyd Weber and don't want to be. I am not Eve Ensler, though I wouldn't mind her bookings. I am not you. I am me, trying to tell my story, tripping over my words, stumbling around, talking about me, my feelings, my observations, and if you can relate, that's great. But this is me, finding my words to get closer to my truth every time I sit down with a pencil and paper.

If you feel the need to say something, stifle it. This is my time, and it really is about me. It's not your opportunity to diminish me. And if something I say triggers a feeling in you, terrific, but I am not you. I am me, with my feelings, my words, not yours. I can listen to your words, watch you dance, sing around, hop around, cry, do whatever you do with an open heart, and I expect the same in return.

This is my process of unraveling, diving deeper, circling down to find my words, my story so that I can write it down. If I feel like screaming, I will. Crying, yep. I'm a storyteller, searching for themes, for plots, for characters, for words, for access to my subconscious to ease the dismal proposition of having to face a new blank page every day.

I'm a storyteller, good at telling a ripping yarn, a tear jerker, an edge-of-your-seat chiller, and my storytelling process has been years in the making, subject to regular revisions and public scrutiny, but still tried and true.

All my life, I've been talking to paper, writing things down, working things out, organizing themes, speaking to no one in particular and connecting with total strangers, people I never see, only meet through letters to the editor. I had to go public, mostly because those people who were supposed to listen didn't have the time to pay attention to a single word I had to say. ⟩

Early

September

Jasmine draped like dust cloths for miles on the back streets heavy in the air, sweet like the promise of a free Thursday afternoon on a day so perfect there is barely a breeze to disturb the eagles nesting in the tree on the road that runs by our house.

I pedal into the afternoon heat, the four o'clock glow that is early September, late summer in Cape May. The sun will set at eight-ish tonight, five minutes earlier than the night before, and tomorrow it will be five minutes earlier still. Five minutes here and there trimmed off our July warm sunlight days.

I pine, knowing how much I'll miss summer and how hard I'll try to convince myself that there is nothing more beautiful than the crisp cool days of autumn. ⟩

p ckets

My left pocket is deep, very deep, and I reach and grab and I still can't get to the bottom. I try again, put my hand in, stretch down so far that as I walk down the street, I list to one side, almost tripping over my own feet, and again, I come up with lint and dust balls and last year's taxi receipts. I come up short.

It's a good thing I'm not a kangaroo. I was raised never to put anything in my pockets. Ladies don't do that. Ladies who stuff wallets, gloves, tissues, eyeglasses and small, but deadly firearms in their pockets get unsightly bulges in all the wrong places, and there is nothing worse than a watermelon-sized lump on your butt or thighs.

I am interrupting this story to make a very personal announcement. I think women should have the same rights to stuff their pockets like all those men in tan polyester pants, short-sleeved greasy white shirts, plastic belts, white tube socks and brown sandals. You know, the guys with mashed potato bellies and pasty, too soft skin; those guys carrying a three days of no shampoo, shower or shave stench. Those guys who look like they just might be pedophiles. Those guys who stuff their greasy, fat leatherette wallets—full of singles and TV dinner coupons—and key rings deep in their front left pockets. The bulge slaps and bounces against their legs, just about mid-thigh.

I wonder if those guys get holes in their pockets?

There's a hole in my never-stuffed pockets. Probably because I put my keys in there once. Only once. I'm not lying, and now, I can't even sew up this hole. It's not on the seam. It's a puncture wound, and the place where my fingers want to go. I poke and prod, a mindless moving meditation, and the hole grows and grows, pulls and shreds. But there's one good thing. If I put sand or bread crumbs or jelly beans or pebbles in my pocket and then walked and walked and walked, I'd always be able to find my way home. ☽

Under

Under the bed, there's a ladder, folded flat, laying under my husband. Boxes under me, full of party supplies, gift wrap and photos taken here and there of them and us and him and her, hastily flipped through, passed around, boxed up and preserved for history.

Whose history?

The

My best friend tells me what I wore for sixth grade graduation, what we did on the trip to Washington, D.C., the second grade classmate who blew his nose into a piece of loose-leaf paper and made me cry. I trust her to remember all the big and little people, what I did on my summer vacations, where I was the day Kennedy was shot and the day Neil Armstrong landed on the moon.

That's why I sleep on my photos. Someone once told me that if I wanted to remember anything, I should put it under my pillow and it would burn into my memory, never to be erased.

Bed

Baloney.

All these years of sleeping over my family photos, and I still don't remember much of anything that would make me believe I lived the life my mother said I lived. ⟩

PINS

NEEDLES

Five minutes ago, a porcupine just walked into the room, not all spiny and angry. Its quills were lying flat, but I got the sense that one wrong move and that porcupine would be a pin cushion in ten seconds flat—one charging, snapping, sticking, ornery character with a major attitude.

You know what made this situation all the more difficult? I don't have a clue about what it is that might rub a porcupine the wrong way. I don't know what porcupines eat or what and when they like to eat. I don't know if they like take-out or home-cooked. I don't know if they prefer to eat on china or paper plates, and who knows if they have any food allergies. I don't know if they prefer wine, beer, soda, water, coffee, tea or fruit juice.

So, I'm playing a guessing game here, moving real slow, not making any sudden, jerky movements, opening this, pouring that and cooking up a choice of entrees. I probably should have called the World Wildlife Fund or the Bronx Zoo before I started pulling out all my pots and pans and defrosting a roast, but I didn't want to seem like anything other than a generous and gracious host. I mean, how many times will I get a porcupine stopping by for dinner?

Still, he could have called first, and he should have asked me if I was busy. But no. He's never read Emily Post. So now, I'm sitting here, cooking, serving, coaxing and treading carefully, trying not to ruffle any quills so I can get through another day. ❯

I don't have a clue, an idea, an inkling, a glimmer, a suspicion, any indication.

But I have a Thesaurus packed with words to define— but not quite precisely—what I don't know, grasp, comprehend, fathom, ken, perceive, understand.

So I log-on, surf the Net, hit help and search and search and search, and still at high noon on a bright summer's day, I'm stumbling in the dark. ❩

WHAT

What if

What if there was no boogeyman in the closet, ever?

What if there were no sounds that go bump in the night and wake me and get me wondering if that crash, slam, bump is the beginning of the end or our first ever encounter with original sin?

What if Chicken Little never said the sky is falling and never put into my head the notion that you can get bopped in the noggin just stepping out your front door?

What if all the elevator inspectors did their jobs well enough to be named employees of the day, week, month and year?

What if what goes up didn't have to come down, but could soar higher and higher?

What if we were all really created in God's image? How would we be able to tell one long dirty-blonde haired, blue-eyed person in a robe from another?

What if nail polish didn't chip?

What if the light stayed on in the refrigerator after you closed the door? Would the milk go sour extra fast?

What if there was no inertia? No cause and effect? No random order of the universe?

What if there was nothing that really scared me, including myself? ☽

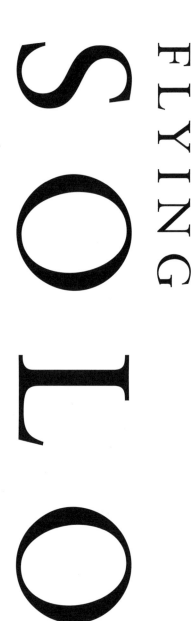

FLYING SOLO

I didn't bring you a present. Sorry.

I came alone, empty-handed, but watered and fed, and designer dressed—bra, panties, trousers, belt, shirt, jacket, handbag, watch, necklace, earrings and shoes—just me.

I am clean, showered, buffed, polished, oiled, patted dry, flossed, brushed, Q-Tipped, manicured, pedicured, coiffed, madeup, parked on the right side of the street and eager to please.

I hope that's okay.)

RED, WHITE &
BOO-HOO

Sunday morning, I make breakfast: scones, egg and bacon omelets, coffee—regular for you, decaf for me—no milk, black and strong from somewhere in Africa.

We chew and sip from sturdy Polish pottery mugs, gulping vitamins, this prescription and that. Quiet, focused on our plates, flipping through the Sunday Magazine, Arts and Leisure, Travel and Sunday Style sections of the *New York Times*, we studiously avoid the front page.

Stuffed, we shuffle to the sofa in bathrobes and slippers, slurping steaming coffee. I grab the remote, and we click on *Meet the Press*. Speaker of this, representative from that, foreign correspondents over there, partisan political advisors, spin doctors, newly elected enemies and allies, queens, kings, despots, potentates, generals going and generals coming back.

I rant. I rave. I ponder. I reach for the tissues. It's my country, and I'll cry if I want to. God knows, this is my one constitutional right that's not threatened yet. ❯

august 2004

This is a summer of atmospheric turbulence, of disturbances in the force, of prayers unanswered, of a cratered moon surrounded by rings and of hurricanes suspended over the Atlantic like Satan's sword.

The moon seems unable to spin on its axis, stuck in the center of the sky like some second-grader's papier-maché clump from a solar system diorama—no Pluto. There's talk that it's not a planet, how sad.

The earth is moving around the sun. I saw it creep up over the horizon at dawn. But the air's not warming to a hazy, hot, humid beach day. I suspect this is the work of some cosmic plumbing problem, clogged filters, leaky pipes, dripping until fire is smoke.

I look for the silver lining in the 70-degree temperature, low-lying clouds, clammy breeze and smog. Ah-ha! The cellulite fairy has come to my rescue. It's a miniature golf, not a beach day, so I won't have to wear my bathing suit and suck in my stomach all day. ⟩

Chick-Lit

Chapter One

Talk, talk, talk. That's my mother, Ernestine, and my best friend, Julia. Do they ever listen? Never. Between the two of them, it's a good thing that ears don't wear out, or I'd be on my ninetieth set of replacement parts.

I mean, if I told you my eleventh grade English teacher, Ms. Butler, was ruining my life, shattering my reputation as an underachiever, you'd say, "Alice, tell me everything. I'm here to listen." But my mom and Julia...ugh!

This big mess with Butler started three weeks ago. She came into class in a foul mood. I figured she had a hangover. I mean, only heavy drinking could get any sane person to sleep with her husband. He's Principal Howard.

And that's another thing.

Butler and Howard seem to think we don't know they're married. Okay, they don't have the same last name and barely talk to each other while they're in school, but they live in town. We see them driving home together and all over the place. Duh! So on this Monday when Butler was grinchier than any other Monday, she came in, looked at us and crumpled a little like a snowman when the sun is high, said, "Write about what you had for breakfast. You have thirty minutes, and make it interesting."

Blair and Melissa, the two popular girls freaked, their hands shot up in the air and they whined, "Ms. Butler, Ms. Butler, OOOOOOOH, Ms. Butler." You see, popular girls don't eat breakfast, or at least that's what they say. It's not cool. Butler let them whine for a few minutes. I thought Blair was going to cry, and she kept shooting these pathetic looks at Adam, her football player boyfriend who looks like he eats half a cow every morning.

Finally, Butler gave Blair and Melissa this look that would have flattened Darth Vader and said, "Use your imagination. I assume you have one."

So everyone in the class wrote, and me, Alice, I had a great story to tell.

Breakfast is always an adventure in my house. Ernestine Dearest insists on cooking something, which is a bad idea, because she's doing too many things to keep an eye on the burners, and breakfast is always extra crispy. This morning, it was a blackened pancake shaped like the African continent. I smothered it in maple syrup and ate it. I am not a popular girl, so when hunger calls, I answer.

Friday, Butler was smiling at me—which looked like a bad gas grimace on her face—when I walked into class. My skin crawled. I sat, twitching, along with everyone else around me. Finally, she spoke. "What a surprise," Butler oozed. "Your breakfast essays were good. One of them earned an A+."

Kathy, who thinks she's channeling Bob Dylan or some beat poet, sat up straight and smiled right into Butler's eyes. She was just about to reach out and grab the paper Butler was holding out until the dorkiest 11th grade English teacher in the history of education plopped the paper and half of her skinny butt on my desk.

"Good work, Alice," was the last thing I heard. Butler launched into a ten-minute preach on how every-one in class should be as creative and write as well as I do. My life was over. This kind of praise would not earn me an invite to Joey Gianni's Texas Hold 'Em Party. It would get me a lot of sneers, laughs, pokes in the ribs and lockers opening in my face.

Things only got worse when I got home. I told my mother, and Ernestine Dearest almost cried. Then she started talking. "I always wanted to be a writer," she gushed, "and now here you are living my dream. It's not an easy life. That's for sure. But your dad and I will support you, even if it takes a few years for you to get a job in journalism or your first book deal after college. And we have to find the right college, somewhere creative, but structured. That's what it takes to be really great, and I know you can be great...."

She went on, and I tuned out. What is wrong with this woman? I wrote one miserable, okay A+ essay. I didn't win the Pulitzer Prize. I tuned back in when she offered to take me shopping. Then tuned out again. Whatever we bought would always be the sweater/pants /shoes/blouse/bag/etc. we bought Alice for her A+ essay, and I'd have to listen to all the praise again, followed by "well, you can only imagine our surprise and disappointment when she never delivered another paper like that. We just don't know what to do anymore, etc., etc."

I could feel myself deflating just thinking about that speech. Mom kept talking. I grabbed the car keys, a bottle of OJ, my pig apron and schlumped toward the front door. "Mom," I bellowed. "I'm going to work."

"Okay, sweetie," she crooned. "I can't wait until your father gets home. Oh, I'm just bursting…"

I didn't hear the rest.

Chapter Two

I work on Friday nights and Saturday from 9 a.m. to 6 p.m. at Porky's. That's why I have an extremely uncool pig apron and headband with pig ears. GROSS!

The 200-year-old goon who owns the place fell in love with those *Porky's* movies and still thinks he's in high school. The pay stinks. The tips do too. Seriously cheap kids from my school come in, squeeze in a booth and drink sodas and coffees for hours and leave zero! But the pitifully small amount of cold, hard cash does pay for distressed jeans and nail tips, which my mother refuses to fund because they are not organic. She is so 1960s, and I mean that in the bad way.

"You're late," belched Mr. Porky from behind the cash register. "Put on your apron and take booth seven. They've been waiting for hours."

Just before sticking a pencil behind my ear, I stopped in my tracks, nearly skidding to a broken leg on a dead home fry. NO! Butler, Howard and another couple that looked too happening to be their friends were sitting at booth seven and looked like hungry wolves waiting for the big kill.

"Please," I flung myself on the cash register. "Send someone else to that table. I'll wash dishes. I'll take the counter. I'll clean the restrooms."

"Seven or you're fired," Mr. Porky said, sliding a greasy $20 in the till and a toothpick in his pie hole.

My only hope was to look down and pray that Butler and Howard didn't recognize me. It wasn't much of a hope. I didn't have a bag over my head or anything.

"Alice," Butler said, all smiles. "I didn't know you worked here."

She was probably the only person in the civilized world who didn't. "Yes," I said, "saving for college." Please, whatever saint or god or karmic force protects geeky teenagers having the worst day of their lives, I silently begged, don't let Butler start talking about the burnt, African pancake essay.

Saved by the guy in Diesel jeans and a leather jacket.

"I'll have a burger with fries, medium rare," he said, no chit-chat, and I thought I heard his stomach growl.

They all ordered the same thing. Butler added a milkshake. Mmmm, eating for two? Butler and Howard doing the nasty? I almost gagged.

I brought the drinks, food, then coffee, two desserts—for the happening guy and his very skinny date, wife, sister, who knew—and then one of those plastic American Express folders with the check.

"This one's on me, Jim," the leather jacket guy said and grabbed the folder.

Principal Howard's name is Jim. I didn't need to know that. "No, Brad," he said. "Even on a teacher's salary, I have enough cash to split the check."

He opened the folder, put in $25 and took Butler's hand and helped her out of the booth. Another $25 from the other two, and I'd still get a stingy tip. Figures. I left them to fight it out and turned to another table, four fat guys who seemed to be training for the eating Olympics. I took their dessert order and turned around again. The guy in the leather jacket was walking out the door, slipping something in his pocket. I picked up the check folder. Empty.

Hey! I almost yelled, but figured Mr. Porky would grab me and a gun, and run after and tackle the four of them. Couldn't happen. I'd never be able to go to school again if my boss and I called my teacher, my principal and their friends thieves. Well, some of the kids might call me a hero, but the parents, faculty, schoolboard, no. This wouldn't be good. ❱

Some Inspiration

My first story was published in my high school literary magazine; my second in my college magazine. The pages were out of sequence. No one seemed to notice. I was ready to die. The year I turned nineteen, I took to writing long, thoughtful letters to everyone I knew, mostly explaining what I knew about life and how I had proof everything they were doing was wrong. I was a peach—although other people might substitute another word—and I thought I was a writer, which gave me permission to say anything on paper, and I thought everything I was saying was pure genius.

Until.

I took a poetry course with Armand Schwerner at CUNY: College of Staten Island. He was pretty aggressive in his criticism of everything I'd ever written before and introduced me and the entire class of twenty-year-olds smitten with eschewing punctuation and capitalization to automatic writing. Armand came into class with an egg timer and instructed us to open our notebooks, to pick up our pens, and once he turned over the egg timer, to start writing and not to stop until all the sand had run down. I wrote some great stuff in that class.

My first journaling class was with Morty Schiff, also at the College of Staten Island. We wrote and talked about what we wrote, and Morty made comments in the margins of our spiral-bound notebooks—all of mine were aqua blue. That year, I wrote a play and a book, and started feeling like I was on the road to becoming a writer.

Twenty-five years later, I was moving and I found those notebooks. My husband, Geoff, and I read through every one of them and cried. Not because my writing was so brilliant or my stories so sad, but because Morty's comments were so insightful and caring. A few days later, I bumped into Morty at a restaurant in New York City and told him about finding the notebooks and my husband's reaction to reading his margin notes: "I wish I had had one teacher who was this thoughtful when I was in school."

About ten years ago, I was working on a client project with government connections. Kenneth Starr was running rampant in Washington, D.C., seizing employees' and consultants' files. I burnt all my journals. My reasoning: if any government agent came and locked up my file cabinets because of a client's malfeasance, anyone who read those journals would think I was nuts, and it was good to unload all that baggage anyway.

Not really.

I picked up an old copy of *Writing Down The Bones* by Natalie Goldberg and then *The Artist's Way* by Julia Cameron with Mark Bryan. I started writing whatever I wanted to write again—no editing, no judgments—and started on my road to becoming a writer again. ☽

How *to* Sleepwrite
Bedtime Stories

Every writer has his or her own writing rituals. If you're writing to free your mind and fall asleep, ready to wake up with plenty of creative get-up-and-go the next day, I'd suggest sleepwriting. Please try some of these simple tips.

1. Get ready for bed. Walk the dog, lock all the doors, turn off all the lights, the TV, stereo and other appliances, and do everything you have to do to secure your living space. Wash your face, brush your teeth, put on your PJs and do whatever else you usually do before turning in.

2. Have a pen or pencil and a notebook that will fit comfortably in your hand at your side of the bed. You don't want anything too large or heavy.

3. Get your pillows plumped so that you can sit comfortably in bed.

4. Turn off any overhead lights and set any alarms that need to be set. Once you start writing, you don't want to have to think about any other responsibilities or getting out of bed.

5. Sit down on the side of your bed and take a few cleansing breathes.

6. Pick up your notebook and pen or pencil.

7. Slip between the sheets, leaning against your pillow, knees up if that makes it comfortable to support your notebook. (Sometimes, I perch on the side of the bed, feet resting on the bed frame.)

8. Start writing the first words that come into your head—even if they are "cabbage grows in my basement" or something worse—and don't stop until you've completed three pages. Let your mind take your hand where it wants to go for three pages. Don't worry if none of what you're writing seems to make sense. Just keep writing.

9. At the end of your third page, put down your pen or pencil, close your notebook, place it on your bedside table, turn off the light and lie down.

10. Sleep.

When I went back to read five years of notebooks in order to select stories for this book, most of my stories concluded in unreadable chicken-scratch. By the end of that third page, I was falling asleep before I'd even finished the last sentence.

Thanks for reading. Want to earn your ZZZZZZZs? Please give sleepwriting a try. It's fun, rewarding and yields great benefits. I'd love to hear about your progress. Please go to sleepwriters@greatlittlebooksllc.com to learn how to submit your stories for possible publication in our next edition of *Bedtimes Stories*.

Thank You

First and always, Geoff Worton, my love and my heart; Linda Dini Jenkins who has been my buddy since I was six and was there for me through every step of this project—including the dazzling jacket copy; Gail Kearns, my friend for over thirty-five years and the one who convinced me to go to BEA, encouraged me to launch my own company and guided me through the birthing of this book; Lucy Levenson, Gail's business partner, and a key driver behind Great Little Books; Carlos Pion for his breathtaking book design, spectacular, whimsical cover illustration and the spirit to follow his vision; Dom Rodi, a brilliant artist and an even better friend, for a fabulous company logo; Rosemarie Nardone, Agnes Nardone and Teresa Kelly for the promotional pillows; Melissa Thogode, Suzanne Lucas and Laura Thogode for help with my marketing kits; Rochelle Udell, who in her brilliant Foreword does a better job of explaining what I'm saying in this book than I ever could; and Jesse Kornbluth, Ed Begley, Jr., Kathleen Rooney, Roz Pelcyger, Noelle Hannon, Caren Lissner, Julie Morgenstern and Anthony Amatullo for jacket quotes that so "got what this book is about" they made me cry.

Praise *for* Bedtime Stories

"I enjoyed every delicious page of Barbara Worton's book, *Bedtimes Stories*, but also found it deeply disturbing, since she writes better half-asleep than I do fully awake."
—*Ed Begley. Jr., Actor and Activist*

"Not just any small press could get away with calling itself Great Little Books, but their first release, the curious and wonderful *Bedtime Stories* by Barbara Worton, proves that they can deliver the goods."
—*Kathleen Rooney, Publisher, Rose Metal Press*

"These are not really stories. Nor are they likely to soothe an overtired child. They're something else—gossamer, appealing, annoying. And insistent. They jab away at your resistance."
—*Jesse Kornbluth, Editor, HeadButler.com*

"These little stories are the perfect bedtime treat to lull your mind to rest after the haste of the day. Barbara Worton has captured the true essence of effective time management by redefining the possibilities of our last moments before slipping into sleep."
—*Julie Morgenstern, Author,* Time Management from the Inside Out

"*Bedtime Stories* welcome you into the wise, sweet, sad and just plain silly stories bouncing through Barbara's sleepy brain. Fast fiction is the hot new genre name for Barbara's sleepwriting. Whatever you might call them, these stories are a joy—even when they challenge you to think outside your own comfort zone. And here's the zinger. Barbara invites you to try sleepwriting and to share your stories for possible publication in the next book in this series."
—*Roz Pelcyger, Director, Glen Rock Public Library, winner 2006* New York Times *Librarian Award*

"Barbara somehow found a way to share her dreams: literally. The silliest, the sweetest and the most profound flights of her considerable imagination are all captured, and given to her reader like a gift. Perfect for the times your brain feels so restless you simply can't relax, or the times you just want to escape ... to take a short trip to dreamland, you just have to turn the page."
—*Vicky Samselski, Assistant Editor, Exit Zero*

"In this delightful presentation of affecting tales and poems, Barbara Worton opens the door to her creative unconscious mind and invites us to enter the magical world of metaphor. Consequently, the reader is seduced into a state of joyful relaxation."
—*Noelle Hannon, PhD, Clinical Psychologist*

"*Bedtime Stories* is a whimsical collection that cuts to the core of life. The stories are a wonderful window to a writer's soul, a private and entertaining conversation with the blank page."

—*Anthony Amatullo, Independent Filmmaker*

"From the quixotic to the practical, Barbara Worton's stories entertain us, make us smile, jar us and bring us to the comforting twilight where our minds are free to explore and surprise us."

—*Caren Lissner, Author and Journalist*

About *the* Author

Barbara Worton has been telling stories since she was a little girl. A lot of those stories have been published in literary, consumer and business publications. Her story, "London Calling," is featured in *Memories of John Lennon*, HarperCollins, November 2005. Her first play, *Brown Shoes Don't Make It,* was based on the music of Frank Zappa and produced at the College of Staten Island. *If I'm Talking, Why Aren't You Listening?*, a play she cowrote with Linda Dini Jenkins, has been staged in New York City, Rutherford, New Jersey, and Boston, Massachusetts, and has received outstanding reviews. Barbara has performed with The Theater Within, founded by Alec Rubin and under the direction of Joe Raiola, and is an accomplished public speaker. Since 1991, she has worked as a freelance writer; before that she was an advertising copywriter, book editor and ghostwriter. She lives in Glen Rock and Cape May, New Jersey, with Geoff, her loving husband.